I0823351

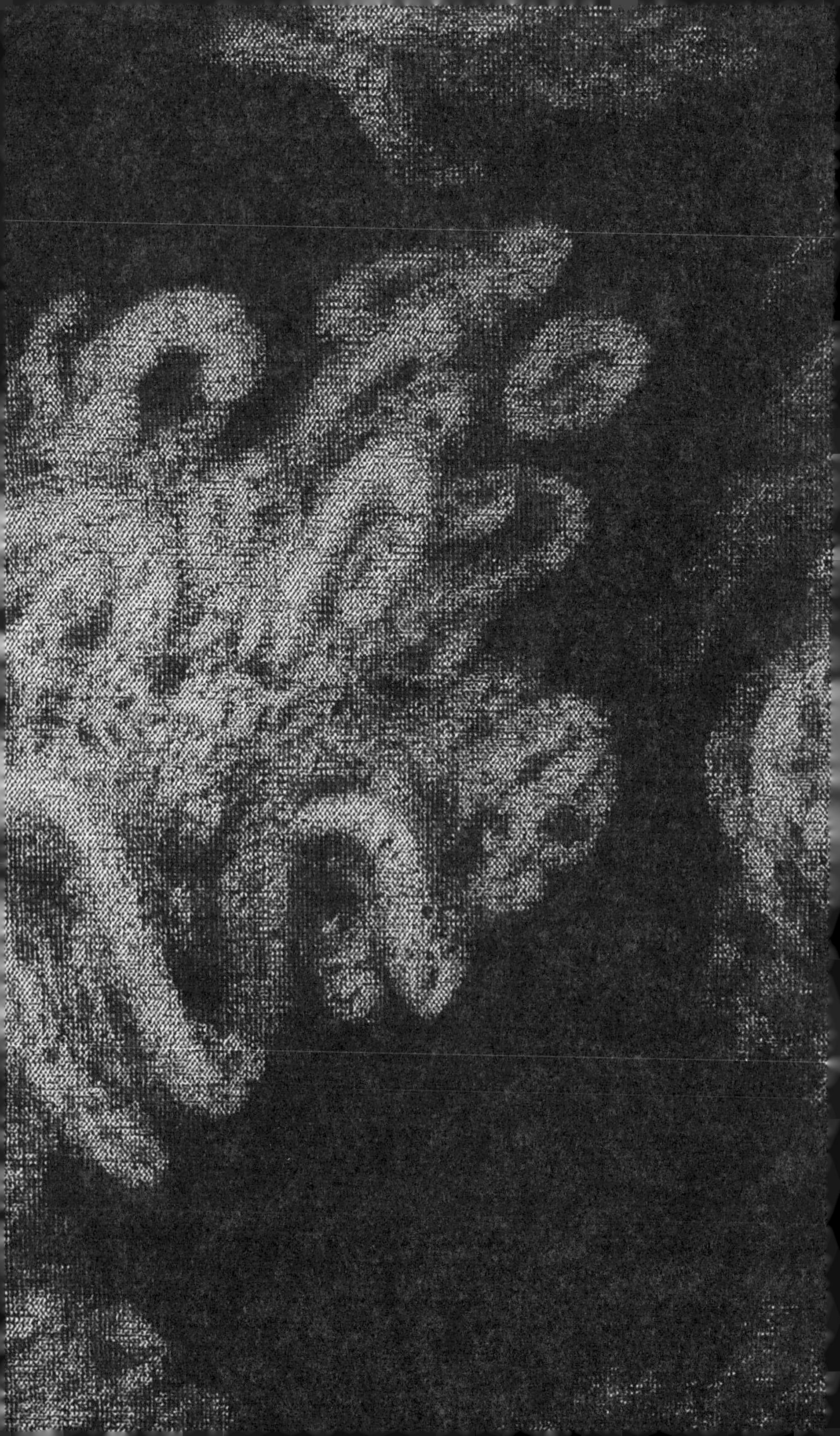

NOTHING AT ALL

OLIVIA TAPIERO

Nothing at All

FOREWORD BY ANNE BOYER

TRANSLATED BY KIT SCHLUTER

NIGHTBOAT BOOKS
NEW YORK

Originally published as *Rien du tout*
by Mémoire d'encrier in 2021

Printed in the United States
ISBN: 978-1-643-62298-9

Cover art, design, and composition by Kit Schluter
Typeset in Bembo Book MT Std

Cataloging-in-publication data is available
from the Library of Congress

Nightboat Books
New York
www.nightboat.org

For my mother, when she was a child

CONTENTS

About *Nothing at All*

ANNE BOYER

Translated with a fierce precision by Kit Schluter, Olivia Tapiero's *Nothing at All* is an urgent, visceral meditation on dissolution. Tapiero's *nothing* is hungry, moody. It gives birth, mutes the stars. It begins as a black hole—a cosmic riddle about claustrophobic emptiness. But the black hole has sisters: the difficult body, the sea, oblivion, the erasures of history. "If every galaxy has a black hole at its center," writes Tapiero, "it is possible that every black hole contains a universe." From this premise, the book itself emerges, born from an orifice that is both the source of this nothing and its frame.

This orifice is witness, and sometimes it is wound, or mouth, or cave, or aperture. It comes both out of the *nothing* and frames it. It is a sensate threshold where being convulses into form and form trembles at its own dissolutions. The orifice "vomit[s] the egg intact," "vomit[s] eyes planets/ women's riddled bodies," expels and ingests with "irresistible viscosity." Colonial, gendered violence is inflicted and resisted there, as the mouth, where tongues are severed, where forced assimilation turns to bile, where the body rebels by expelling what it cannot digest. Jealous gods give birth through their mouths. Hungry animals cry out through them. History is swallowed, as is the present's nauseating banality, "raising awareness about plastic/congratulating diversity committees" and "vomiting every last drop/one vertebrae at a time."

If the black hole is a cosmic manifestation of nothing, its earthly counterpart is the memory hole, carved by colonial erasure. Tracing the ravages of violence and the enduring condition of diasporic life, the "stray bullet" enters the text, piercing through the bodies of the "orphaned ancestors" to cut through time, place. The state's brutality reveals itself as an instrument of inscription. Memory is broken—"Names have been erased along with languages and beaches. Ghost languages, ghost beaches, the shores are eroding and I have nothing to say." The hole is an ambivalent inheritance. Origin, the book decides, is the void.

The circle is the shape at the center of Tapiero's cosmology. To attempt to turn a circle over, to seek a new angle, is to learn each question brings an answer of more of the same. Circles are hypnotic, obsessive, the preferred geometry of mystics and lunatics. A circle is the border of both enlightenment and madness, offers no respite, denies resolution, fucks with fixity, refuses its fill. Yet it is also from this shape that all (or nothing) emerges, from which what can be born, is. The structure of the book—with its spiral expansions, its accruing specificities—stays tightly bound to this Ouroboric form of obsession, the engine of history's repetitions, an abyss which births more abyss.

This unrelenting recursiveness—the total within the nil, and its inverse—promises to unravel meaning and to dissolve the constructed self. The book seizes on this as an invitation and opportunity: "I will not fill the gap." Tapiero refuses to involve the text in the cynical production of sense, but she does not soften senselessness's terror. Her work layers and iterates and rotates its central figure (nothing, hole, mouth, wound, void) as an uneasy method of comprehension. This method is not without its ambivalence:

> What I've seen accumulates in the depths of my body, the strata pile up, interlock, sediment, my bones are engraved with lies. I repeat that there is no origin, to convince myself: a gesticulation in an indeterminate plasma. I repeat: I give birth to myself. I repeat it in order to exist, to dissolve in a different way.

Nothing, in Tapiero's book, is ever inert. It is a vital, accruing, distributed process. Everything spins, returns, spans wars, cities, families, fossils, clinics. All is hard, empty, and broken. The book flares up with melancholy and ambivalence. What is salvaged appears only in the low tide's stark reveal, but nothing is here to be restored. This is not a work that seeks to mend, to argue, to prove, to solve. In this world, only the emptiness is worth thinking through. It, alone, does not imitate. The sentences register this tremor of difficult truth. The pain in them dazzles.

Tapiero has written a work terrifying in its scope, exhilarating and ambitious. Its propositions are not given easily. Its terrain is simultaneously cosmic, somatic, and historical, a convergence of scales and registers that defies neat categories. Its catharsis is an abject, emetic purging. This is a text rich with the staggering vitality of self-annihilation and self-birth, refusing while singing of "the sapped memory, a desirous dislocation … the stars' collapsed hearts."

"Emptiness," writes Tapiero "only has value when it's a man who speaks of it—preferably a limp humanist… *we, the others, aren't allowed metaphysics*." And yet whether or not we are allowed them, metaphysics exist, exerting their invisible force even on those to whom their vocabularies are denied. All the relentless, necessary recreating happens underneath the event horizon, here in the *something* that is trapped in the *nothing* outside of which nothing else could be known. With tears "dragged to Delphi," Tapiero's are delinquent metaphysics—vatic and resolute.

NOTHING AT ALL

BLACK HOLE

an event horizon is when a woman collapses in on herself

NIKKI WALLSCHLAEGER

It seems to me that we understand
the world better if we tremble with it.

ÉDOUARD GLISSANT

THE FIRST ORIFICE opens to the world: eye, flower, scream. Sea anemone, heart valve. A fissure of light in the galactic void.

I retrace the spiral that led me into nothingness. I howl under the stars, seeking your eye, the better to remove myself. If you see me, I disappear. They'll burn me alive and pick up a black stone from my ashes. Take it in your hands, press it against that taut place between your ear and your jaw, listen: there's nothing.

It's nothing.

I go on, knowing that I'll have to let part of myself die. That this murder, inexhaustibly repeated, lies at the heart of a secret pact, an aimlessness whose unknown timbre will infuse my voice. I return to a low frequency, melting into the seagulls' calls, the branches knocking against each other. My whole life will have been this attempt to dissolve; that's how the heart reveals itself: the mouth devours the fruit's flesh, decomposition returns it to the earth. That's how the core becomes apparent.

At the bottom of the sea, there are living fossils—their bodies are all we know of prehistoric times. The composition of these organisms is optimal; it hasn't needed to change for millennia. There is a brutal, miraculous simplicity to it: everything organizes itself around the mouth. Eyes sit around the mouth like a crown, taking the place of lips, and a toothed mouth lies between the legs; they see in the dark, and their little legs crush their food to push it inside. Once a year, during a full moon, the fossils travel to the shore to reproduce. Scientists wait for them there, then capture about 500,000 of them. With a syringe, they draw blood from the fossils' hearts in order to identify the active pathogens in pharmaceutical solutions. Upon contact with the fossils' blood, any foreign body contaminating the solution turns phosphorescent, easily detectable. Once the operation is complete, the ancient creatures are released back into the water—half of them survive this abduction; within two to three weeks, the rest are dead.

I wanted to swallow the sun, to absorb the desired bodies, to hold the sea in my eyes without mourning its shores. It's an appetite that overwhelms me—a love so big for the living that grief becomes inconsolable. I end up wanting to disappear, to wall in my hunger and this excessive, suffocating love, a tidal wave that scares me into lying here stunned in the same room for days, beginning nothing, so that all may remain pregnant, as if swollen with light.

For the first time, the horizon collapses on itself and the time of appetite coincides with that of history, of the years we have left, of an urgency stripped of a tomorrow. I continue to put one foot in front of the other, as if to imitate the era when we still couldn't see the end of the road. Hunger trails me like a shadow.

Humans have imposed their rhythm on the world as on the world's destruction. I stop talking, smooth out my skirt and imagine an apocalypse to put limits on a storyline, to accelerate the collapse, to do something abrupt. Many of us have coveted the end times, a loud punishment, a nasty old spanking, a disastrous, pornographic feast. I learn to mistrust what makes no sound as it empties the night of its stars, what passes by in silence, like a garden snake, or a law.

This shore is condemned: nothing can be projected upon it. The town is built on a swamp that fills with the salt of rising tides, birds resting on the rocks, humans don't live here, they rent, they sell, they run away from the anticipated flooding of their vacation homes. Yesterday I pissed in these dunes, ran over the pebbles of this beach, the big pier that stretches off toward the horizon, the currents, their clamor, stuck my finger into some jellyfish that had washed ashore, almost cried out with the seagulls, my head thrown back between the waves and the sky, but I didn't dare.

For a long time, I wanted to die. I thought about death every day. This morning I looked out at the sea and knew, in my gut, that this death I'd dreamt was only a way to trace the contours of my body. A scission to be born. The waves sparkled, still greyed out in the light of dawn, and I thought to myself that I could stay there, laid out on a rock, my face offered up to the sun, until the tide cloaked and engulfed me. It was a quiet form of happiness that I wanted to inhabit, even if it washed me away. Serene torpor tames death. And it's always been toward death that I've gravitated, not to flee pain, not because I have no hope for the world, but to let myself melt into this joy, to a state of total presence, of dissolution. A wild dog came running toward me, startled me, saved me.

Some lives are organized around absences, like the galaxies that form around black holes. I drink until I black out to gain access to this space, but I am what ends up emptying out, my heart ripped from my center. Sweat, an acrid smell. My tailbone is crushed, rainfall streams down my face. I remember almost nothing. Entire segments, consumed. Forgetting is protection, a keloid incapable of smoothing out the wounded surface. I read somewhere that if every galaxy has a black hole at its center, it's possible that every black hole contains a universe. Can we fall into a hole of memory, fall so far that we sink into a forgetfulness that doesn't belong to us?

I'm carrying something. Maybe a tumor, a child, an idea, a serious illness, or a talented little dog. A grief, a scream, a mutation. It's still too early to tell. It's ugly and cumbersome. It's getting bigger, it's growing, I can already see myself in shed skin, in an eggshell, in a placenta. It's like that sickness that makes patients imagine colorful worms squirming under their skin, then squeezing out of their pores. I'd love to give the parasite a name, but I only see my face. Pretty soon this thing will occupy the majority of my body, it will break out of my skin, leaving behind what is no longer me.

Something will grow there, between appetite and ambition.

I shiver in multiple spectres. I try to tell you about the pain that has frozen like a fat bug, blinded by daylight. I stuck my arms into the earth, protected the spaces between the nail and the skin. I didn't cry at first—the foreign bodies remained in my eyes, I kept watching the sea, guessed their corpses and their gardens, the century absorbed in a wheeze. Here, absence is what makes the place. The drowned have no faces, and the more the vacationers pile into town, the more it seems haunted, detached from itself.

I am bound by friendship to everything around me. Epiphany is relational. I've felt it while reading as I've felt it in a forest, hearing strangers talk to me until the night turned white, or on acid, bowled over by a mountain streaming with roots. The experience of relation dissolves me. It's the only form of disappearance that remains untouched, that isn't violence or erasure. A decolonial disappearance.

There are dead zones at the bottom of the sea as there are at the heart of the body. Inaccessible sites, hypoxemic and numb. Places of forgetting, anesthesia. That's where I'm writing you from. That's what writes inside me. It's a difficult, lonely place, a place that searches without coming to a conclusion, and where one can cite nothing, where one can hardly breathe.

Each pain resembles every other, they converge in anonymity: every lack has the same grey taste tingling after loss. I dig into other bodies to discover my wound, and at night the plants turn pale. So I stay here.

I could spend the rest of my life here, gathering seashells. Running back to the far side of childhood.

The drowned sink to the bottom of the sea, their outstretched arms are the algae of this world. Disheveled mouth-coral, the eye rolled back on the other side of the surface, where sunlight quakes, where skin burns, where salt encrusts cries.

How many faces still need to be erased? I hope that life outlives us, that the dams break, that the water finds its course.

I hid my hopes at the bottom of oceanic abysses, alongside the other monsters. The circle closes behind my heels. I prepare myself to lose your voice.

My thumb slides over the screen and time slides like my pupil over the world and this thing in my throat keeps getting bigger. When I emerge from the earth, my organs are mixed up: my mouth is a dazzled eye, my tongue a shorebird, my tongue a disguised eel, I shave my head, I buy myself a blue wig, my lips trace the words of a lost song, my gums bleed, I have a secret, like a stringy piece of meat clenched between teeth, every night I lose my teeth and dream about hotel rooms and makeup in neon lights. The cyborg's desire has been implanted under my skin. I want to dematerialize. Dematerialize narration. Erase myself, again. To reach the core. But the path of loss has been traced.

I am one of those who press machines to their hearts to send out signals, to get in contact with the world outside, to multiply faces until they touch the resistant nothingness. My mouth is full of crushed landscapes. The heart looks for a little disaster in order to expand. It won't cry out at injustice—it will only ask us to bury it in the garden alongside the animals.

I watch videos, watch mouths, whispering mouths, mouths eating live octopi, honeycombs, udon noodles, sauced meat, I watch the noisy mouths, I consume the mouths that consume, I'm an ouroboros machine, an absolute orifice. Language and food come in and out through the mouth, entering and exiting with an irresistible viscosity. There's almost nothing left under human skin. Sometimes it sparks, sometimes a sentence returns like a cut, sometimes something is reflected on the sea's surface.

The sea is a tomb and mouths blossom all over me, unfurling in petals on my palms, my breasts, my throat, my sex. The void opens to the sky and bodies beget themselves like hunger, in forests and hospital rooms. I left a scream in your black room. The back of my neck still retains your belly's warmth, my throat the clenching of your voice. There are houses made for screaming, houses of cracked earth, that were built along the riverbanks, that wash away with every flood.

On the Russian front, at the beginning of the last century, a man observed the arced paths of projectiles; by studying an as-yet-unsolved equation, he was able to describe the curvature of rays of light and calculate the distortion of space-time that indicates the existence of black holes. We glean their existence from the behavior of surrounding bodies, by the lines traced by what has been swallowed whole. The core remains unknown to us, we deduce it from its hunger, from the radiant variation of disappearing matter. There is only one way out before you're dragged across the inner horizon: follow a spiral course, in the direction opposite the black hole's rotation.

Some bubbles foam up on the sand, lives digging out a refuge under the soles of my feet. I pick up the shell of a dead sea urchin, symmetric calcite I'd love to place on my tongue. Later on, I hold it up to my face to look closely at its orifice. An urchin's mouth is in direct contact with its substratum. A crown of nerves surrounds it. The animal feeds on algae, mollusks, sponges, and carrion. It also uses its mouth to dig into stone and craft itself a refuge, a miniature cave. We use the word *enfumades* to refer to those operations the French army used in Algeria, where they grouped natives in caves, then set fires at their mouths, so that everyone inside would die of suffocation. *Enfumade*: emptying out a surplus of vitality, the untamable or unaddressed. I roll a joint and savor it slowly, letting its burn swirl around my lungs, then swell inside my mouth. I play around, blowing little smoke rings into the empty room. I smoke until I can't tell if I'm the sea urchin, the cave, or the soldier.

Listen: I'm not trying to fix anything, to dig up proof, I'm not trying to reimagine a history for myself, to return to some origin. I sing the sapped memory, a desirous dislocation, sing the stars' collapsed hearts, the absolute horizon of a black hole distorting space-time, I sing orgasm and dispossession. The glaciers melt, releasing ancient bacteria. At low tide, we discover the bodies of the drowned. I want to write at low tide.

NOW YOU SAY NOTHING

I feared for my jaw and tongue
I assumed that language was a symptom of disease

ANNE BOYER

I will open my mouth and others will scream.

NATHANAËL

THE WINDOWS ARE OPEN—gusts and tides sweep through the house as the nation shuts its doors. At the borders, vigilance is redoubled, bodies wreck themselves against freshly erected walls. It's the same bullet that slaughters them, a stray bullet that cuts through the bodies of my orphaned ancestors to pierce from one century into the next, endlessly, from Oran to Oka, from Harlem to Nanjing, from Fez to Tijuana, from Auschwitz to Lesbos, from Flint to Fez, from Calais to San Juan. And everywhere, the landscapes it crosses are a form of writing.

The hole crept up on me like an intimacy. I annihilate myself in a glance, a remark, a question. I hide my diagnoses under the mattress, next to the stains of menstrual blood, nightmares, and yellow clouds of mold. The flowers have closed again, a pervasiveness in the air. Try as you may to grasp the world, you end up saying nothing at all. Maybe I'll end up saying nothing at all. Until then, I'll sink like a splinter into the century, gorging myself on creams and carcasses, tasting nothing. I fear what might attempt to situate me. I swam to the center of the lake, my arms coursing with electric shocks. A withdrawal effect. I'm not begging for refuge but for risk run, the fragile uncertainty, the beating bellies of hesitant lives. I'll follow nothing but hunger. I evacuate. I piss hard, with a stream more powerful than myself. Every night I dream of this uncontrollable piss, a flow that passes through me, overflowing me, ejaculating me.

All objects gravitate toward an abyss, caught up in the same fall. Once beyond the horizon, a body is irresistibly drawn toward the force that ultimately crushes it. Some say *depression*, others *capitalism*, *colonialism*, *patriarchy*. Puppets have vampirized *self-care*. The *self* has become a product, state property, the luxury of kings and the mirage of fools. You say autonomy and I hear capital. The doctor ups my prescription, telling me to continue taking my pills every night.

Madness: beyond a certain threshold, there's no return. Once you've passed the intermediate zone, you're inevitably dragged into the core. All ground cracks under my feet. I approach the horizon, ready to cross over without noticing. I emit an irregular light, and you still can't tell that the star's flickering denotes the play of distance, that these shiny objects are nothing but stellar corpses, swept up in a dance with invisible depth.

I dug into my flesh to excise the voices that haunt it—I undid myself, burned down my house, cried wolf and wept at the bottom of the sea; my hair fell out, my nails breaking on the ramparts. I danced in quicksand, learned the final solitude and the anonymity of sap, understood that survival cannot be cleansed by the cruelties that enable it, that rare is the love which is not a refusal to stand, alone together, between the molts and deaths that define our stammered gestures.

My name slaughters me. It starts with the belly, which falls away from the rest of my body and becomes as foreign to me as a soft, distant planet. The belly is the only boneless place. Bellies throb. The bellies of hares, birds, cats. I write ligaments to myself, connective tissue to postpone the fall.

Blood clots burn my hips, days shatter my pelvis with hammer blows, the pain resonates in my joints, between pelvis and thigh, then radiates in concentric circles, numbs the legs, pricking the sole of my foot. A doctor talks to me about referred pain, where pain is felt elsewhere than at the source. I wonder if there is even a source for this pain, which I imagine as diasporic, intercontinental. My hip hurts because I have nowhere else to feel it. I hurt for others. I hurt the way others have a word on the tip of their tongue. It's a phantom pain, the call of a long-deserted place.

We pierced the country like a hail of bullets. That's where it breathes, between the living and the dead. I borrow my age from forgotten languages. And the masters, they don't even suspect how poor they are.

My parents told me I shouldn't waste my time learning Arabic, that I was a *hmara* for even thinking about it, that it would do me no good, zero, nada, *walou*. They enrolled me at a French high school, my grandmother's eyes sparkled when she said Paris, and I myself fantasized about courses in great literature, cobblestones and prestigious schools. While I was there, a boy told me I was a nice little *beurette*—I didn't know that word, but it came back to me years later when I heard about the sex film *La Beurette de la Cité*. One porno-colonial image after another. A week after the conquest of Algiers, prostitution was legalized to ensure that the colonists could enjoy themselves to the fullest extent of the law. During the fight for independence, the Algerian resistance was punished with the rape of girls and women.

After the torture and interrogations, after hiding in caves and basements, after the abuse and electric shocks that continued until they forgot their own language, until all that remained were the conqueror's words, their skin could no longer bear any human touch, panic coagulating behind their smiles, so many of them stopped eating. They wandered the hallways, emaciated and unable to bear witness with anything other than their bodies.

I keep returning to the scene. I scratch my hunger into my mother's mirror, I look for my name in your language, this terrain of defeat. A scenario freezes deep in my flesh. I turn the world's weapons against myself, repeat my fables, tear out my stomach. I won't beg for the end of the story.

My grandmother loves the Americans, who, in her eyes, have remained soldiers, saviors, young men straight out of the sky who land in occupied territory, who say *hi there, pretty girl* and drop sticky sweets into her little palms, who teach her to speak English, to say *chewing gum*, to say *God bless America*, to say *freedom*. She eats the sweets as she treads the dirt road between school and home, and collects and chews the used condoms they toss into the fields. I too have long sought sugar in pale eyes, heiress to a displaced desire.

Between the stacks in the high school library, the boy I coveted—blond-haired, blue-eyed, like all those who would follow—told me: *you know, you've got nice lips. Nice dick-sucking lips*. I was glad that he was looking at me.

Nothing whiter than those blue eyes.

I recited the provinces from the history books, the erasures traced in chalk layered inside my mouth. I was taught nothing of the murders buried by these places, nor of the itineraries that led to my being born here, far from the languages that mold my flesh, far from the red lands where, one morning, two women collapsed in a single cry. The nation leaks out between my legs.

I've learned to argue, to write essays and theses. I learned dates by heart under a century at half-mast while my hatred grew without my knowing why. I began to desire out of spite, to seduce out of revenge, at the risk of ending up as prey. I learned your reasons for being able to defend any point of view. I honed this agility, separated words from bodies, as if to approach a certain masculinity: a collaborator's education.

It was a kind of training, being able to pass between worlds. I try to flourish in the irreconcilable. I quickly become the other. It's a way of surviving, of dying differently, perhaps more slowly. Exoticism compresses me to make me readable, desirable.

The compression of matter precedes the collapse of the star's core. It can last for decades, centuries, from corset to career, from maternity to architecture. A woman gives birth on a bed of napalm called a protectorate. From the Maghreb to Indochina, we are taught proper accents, pronunciation that, despite its impeccability, will not rid us of our skin or our riddled bodies. Retraction reacts to compression. A hostile environment. I can't move. Not even out of thirst. So I take care of the hole. I press the right buttons, multiply the windows, numb my exposed neurons. I relish being hollow, keep my eyes open, smoke joints that dry out my mouth, redraw the map of the world with my bed sores.

In the hotel room with heavy curtains, after a rape I couldn't name until years later, he puts his hands on my shoulders. Two heavy tarantulas, thumbs pressed where my collarbones meet my throat, where my breath hesitates to be reborn. I cry silently, not understanding. His mouth comes close to my ear:

now you say nothing

now, forget everything

I speak to you of buried flesh and names that can't be found. I speak to you of the limits of literature, and of its tentacles. What do you want me to say? The premature sacking, the cannibalistic maternity, the coffee the rapist pays for the day after, the colonization of Algeria? Where does the wound begin? I'm trying to find out whose ghost I am. I know how to inhabit other people's childhoods, not this inherited void, not the crossed-out names of those who came before me. I'm ashamed, disarticulated. I repeat the crime the way one learns a lesson.

At your place, I make myself very small. It's a contraction like that of the heart, or of the sex that has given birth. Before the birth of the black hole there is a densified, untenable body.

now, forget everything

Forget Arabic, forget language, having someone else's tongue in your mouth, your tongue forced in, my head caught in huge hands. I wake up soaking wet in the acrid sheets, the bedroom upside down, escaping from a dream against which the texture of the morning seems false. My chest has collapsed, my heart is pounding under my jaw, aching from crushing the sentences I can't manage to say, emerging from a night that's broken my teeth, from the sleep of the vigilant, of the raped, from the backwash of swooning, forgotten things, dislocated gaps of memory rising up from my stomach into my throat, and that's madness, an impossible evacuation, an excess of indecipherable memory in the body,

French fills the mouth

the mouth remains closed

don't talk *with your mouth full*

I learn to vomit

the indigestible the refusal the protectorate,

my native hunger
now you say nothing

The command follows the overstepped border, the fear of revenge, of a call-out, so he orders me to forget, my word will be held against me. Someone has to take the blame. Nothing will be mentioned in the archives, his wife and sons will go on with their lives and I'll choke down the night, renarrate the event, wake up in a panic, my body frozen with fear at the sight of a silhouette that resembles his. I'll smoke, endlessly, having one drink too many. Another story barely exists: only traces, in remote places. It remains to be unearthed, at the risk of disfigurement. Not even forgetting belongs to me, it's named by this other mouth, the mouth is the site of forgetting and forgetting is the site of history and other obediences.

Wearing makeup, my great-aunts iron their dresses and their hair, bursting into laughter in front of the mirrors, dreaming of Brigitte Bardot and Audrey Hepburn, and, in the evening, they take their skin off, polishing their bones in baths of warm milk and blood, while the children outside, lined up in alphabetical order, recite fables stuffed down their throats, and flags sink into their chubby flesh that squeals, still extending from their mothers' wombs.

I wanted so badly to be on the other side and it was only later I understood: when I was riding a guy who asked me if I preferred making love with boys or girls, clearly to latch onto some Sapphic fantasy, I answered that I mistrusted men's fears, suddenly he couldn't get it up anymore, his nakedness had become unbearable for him. Now I cradle those women who weave paths between their anger and the silence of nations. Some women speak to each other. They shout, laugh, spit, cry, pass along provisions, words, whatever it takes to hold on just a little longer. Sometimes they are accomplices, as I still am, no doubt, when I let you guide my hand toward the sorrows you deny yourself.

I can't find faces that look like me. I'm getting ugly and it comforts me. The world is not fit for my excess. The women in my family have been compressed by an impalpable force, the perfectionism of the colonized, the kind anchored in belt blows and memorized texts, the thirst for an unattainable height, constantly postponed. A time bomb, passed down from mother to daughter, eventually exploded in my genes. But be happy, dear, they tell me, thank upward mobility, success and what it crushes, what it hides, what it drives away, and through which mistrusting mouths will accuse me in a word, with good reason.

Diagnoses no longer console me. I read somewhere that emptiness is a bourgeois concept. Later, with you, I understand that emptiness only has value when it's a man who speaks of it—preferably a limp humanist with a grant to write a 500-page book, an Islamophobic cosmopolitan epic, or a novel about some professor's melancholy, an idea of Québécois literature. A friend warns me: *we, the others, aren't allowed metaphysics.*

Mouths, eyes, hands disintegrate. Spines collapse everywhere, the weight of skulls absorbed by numbed thirst. A friend who lives on the other side of the border explains to me that, since the beginning of what she calls "the regime," several of her relatives have fallen ill. After the elections, she herself had her eyelids swollen shut almost completely, as if to protect her from a world in which her eyes would sink and risk taking everything else down with them. She describes to me more serious cases: among her colleagues, the women mostly, there's one who's losing her sight completely, and another who, after having what she took to be a toothache that radiated throughout the bone structure of her face, was diagnosed with necrosis of the jaw. The rotting marrow in her diseased skeleton makes her breath smell like a corpse. Her friend tells me: *They'll be operating on it soon, and it's going to cost a fortune, not to mention the prosthesis she'll need. Can you imagine losing half your face?*

A tarantula unfolds in the pianist's head, its legs entangled in the folds of her brain and slowly tightening, robbing her of her words, in one language then the other, destroying her ability to decipher letters and musical notes, an inextricable mass eating away at her sight, first her left eye, then her right. A week after the diagnosis, she asked me if she hadn't talked too much on the phone, kept the cell pressed too close to her temple, forced her thoughts too far. She told me she was being punished for what she had done, and this guilt was a Catholic, neoliberal fear, a work ethic sculpted by fleeing poverty, austerity, her mother's house and then the house of her husband, who often raped her after the children had been put to bed. At the time of the tumor, she had just named what was wrong, moved to her own place with her dog and her piano. The dog died just after her and the piano disappeared. I found it a year later, on the other side of the border. A building was being evacuated and nobody wanted the instrument. A man was paid to destroy it with a hammer. He was crying. Later, an artist told me about the pianos stored like coffins in the basement of the Palais de Tokyo, pianos without names, without hands, instruments torn from flats with families turned in by neighbors, then deported and murdered. There was the basement of pianos and the basement of the hospital, the basement of our first house and the basement of the first girl I loved, her brothers who had killed a dog and hidden the body. Winds encircle a black core at the heart of my brain, the tides eating away at my shattered memory.

Dying octopuses pinned to steel stretchers squirm in an emergency room. Behind a curtain, a woman is having her left breast removed. Several screens display her heart rate, which is mine. I ask about a sick friend. I learn that they have emptied her out, extracting dead bones from her wrists, her shoulders. She has no organs anymore, no vagina. Not even a window in her room.

I continue to follow the fault lines, the traces of collisions, the swallow's shattered vertebrae, the crumbling strata of the mountain, the earth as red as ashamed cheeks. I carry worlds, rivers, I give birth to flowers and dogs. Birth has filthy hands and dirt under its fingernails.

One of them, the mother or the daughter, always ends up paying the price. Concavity precedes me—that of the starving and the orphan girls. Now is the time to remove myself from the lineage of the holed-out, the martyrs, the sacrificial mothers, the colonized people, the anorexics, the exiles. Now is the time to recognize, in my cry, the confiscation that binds me to those whose fits of rage are the world's appetite.

The hole is passed on in the hearts of women, from mother to daughter, from mouth to mouth. The honey has gone bitter and the flowers have dried up in a ghost town. Bodies contaminated by the centuries' silence.

Other land
Motherland
Fatherland

I'm waiting for the metro to take me to the hospital when a screen tells me that the fascists have won the elections. I watch them congratulate each other, their faces bloated with victory. The pain intensifies around my pelvis, then crawls up my back to the back of my neck. My nerves flare and inflame.

Smotherland

Continents are coming apart in my joints, in my ankles, in my fingers, a weakening of the ligaments, that's what they said. There's an excessive precarity in what binds me to myself and to the world. I sit down on a plastic chair. I wait for someone to call my number at the Ministry of Disintegration.

Between the fractured pelvis and the count of the drownings, between the fruit tree and the abyssal life, I rediscover the first tenderness, that which folds up inside me to lick its blood. I carry a desert as vast as chagrin, and that is where I am host. I move through the invisible parts, it's not exactly a place, more like a plastic film stuck to places, a membrane made of erased lines, of loves without address. To walk through what you can't see is to risk unwitting obedience. I move through the city, heavy as a hand placed over the world, woven of desires, distances, bodies overflowing their itineraries, gouged-eye predictions, maneuvers reproduced by frantic fingers searching for a memory.

In Fez, my grandmother, still a child, feared the scarred faces of the men who had been placed on the front line, the cannon fodder recruited from the French colonies. Still, in the Montreal winter, she regrets her fear, remembers the sadness of those disfigured men when she whimpered in terror as they waved at her on the bus, and then her mother, that orphan from the mountains who threatened her if she didn't behave: *Be careful, I'll hand you over to the Senegalese…* My grandmother tells me this story and cries over her dumplings, so I tell her, *Mamie, you didn't know, you were so little* and she repeats, *but poor things, poor things, after all they've seen…*

Nocturnal neuralgia, stomach ulcers, psychogenic amenorrhea. The axons swell, the muscles knot in the body, which has had to remain on the alert and absorb the shocks. Fanon writes: *this contracture is in reality quite simply the postural accompaniment, the existence in the muscles of the colonized of his rigidity, his reticence, his refusal in the face of colonial authority*. A war breathes under the noise. I settle down with the voices that scratch at my body like daggers in broad daylight.

On the telephone, my aunt's voice reaches me from a douar near Marrakech. She says: *sometimes I hope for war, just so they'll order me to get out, to leave this country.*

It was easy to believe in an image of happiness. The real has bled to death, it's a dull taste, and yet the scene was there, all you had to do was slip into it, embrace excellence, athleticism, grace, good food, and the rites of passage.

A pain in my bones wakes me up, or maybe it's the planes flying over the borders, that sound of death. The wall is secondary. It is built to reflect the climate that creates the idea of the wall. Discourse is what we come up against before washing ashore. But the affected bodies lose their nails, their teeth, poisoned on maps drawn freehand by human fear.

The threat precedes me. The *chkoumoune*, the *shour*, which my grandmother pronounces *zhor* when she tells me about the spells the crumpled spirits impose on those women who attract the evil eye. One morning, in a village where the wind drives people mad, her mother wakes her up screaming, forbidding her to look in the mirror: the *zhor* has disfigured her, her childlike features have drained from the right side of her face. The eyes blended together, the nose moved under the ear, and the mouth slid down along the jaw. She must have upset *the ones below* by throwing out bread or sweeping during the night. The furious mother and the humiliated daughter walked to the village, to meet an elder *fqīh* who lived in a dark and labyrinthine cave. The man spoke Tamazight, a language that had been confiscated from the child, just as Arabic would later be confiscated from me. He asked the daughter and mother to repeat after him. The spirits receded and the child's face returned. Before letting her go, he warned her: a curse will follow you, you and your children. My face is still where it should be. I surround my sleep with gris-gris accumulated from travels and family dinners. My disfigurement takes a different shape. I have to tear off several faces before I find my own. I remove the layers with a blade. And at the center there's nothing.

My pulse quickens, the blood rushes through the currents and degenerate generations, drips from tamed hair and impeccable nails, climbs the Atlas Mountains, then streams down to the center of the earth, which boils and struggles, the center whose fires burn my sternum, my throat, and come back down swallowed, so I open my mouth to say: yes. Yes is a hole, and what is the hole if not my name?

In "1983… (A Merman I Should Turn to Be)," Jimi Hendrix imagines himself as a mermaid escaping from war-torn Vietnam. To save himself, he flees to the bottom of the sea.

so down and down and down and down

My sister's rituals are always linked to objects, their presence, their arrangement. It's her main attachment to the world, the cuddly toys always lined up in the same order, the next day's outfit spread out at the foot of the bed, and then the same lullaby repeated a thousand times before a sleepless night. My sister spent the first months of her life screaming in an orphanage in Ho Chi Minh City. I don't know the story of the woman who gave birth to her, or the cracks of war that ran through her. In my sister, I recognize a frenzy contained by fragile but obstinate barriers. In the family home, one by one, we will work toward our own destruction. Each of us caught up in our own flight, the lightning speed of our thoughts, our compulsive hands, and the fear of the feverish forces that always threaten to rise up by the throat, the gesture, the next slip,

and down and down we go

I hear the key turning in the lock and I don't know if the door will open on this engulfing thousand-year anger, this anger of those who have been silenced, those whose mothers have been silenced, this anger poured out on the daughters, so that they too are silenced. There are fissures that run through centuries and continents, and despite immigration, success upward mobility the American dream, you end up a wreck, depression afflicting the body sprawled out on the Moroccan carpet, in front of the glowing TV, without even the echo of a language or a prayer.

In the house I left behind, my mother is restless, busy, she shuts off, tidies up, constantly smooths the surface until the tension causes new cracks, the reappearance of that impossible hunger, of the panicked look that comes before the gestures, the lists, the cries. A small mechanical dog trips over itself. My sister screams in the bathroom, the door locked from the outside. My sister screams from the orphanage and later on a dealer's sofa, my sister screams on a stretcher, her arms tied and mouth black with charcoal. My mother screams then falls silent, my sister continues screaming, her mouth twisted, gaping, a wound creasing her face that nothing but herself will be able to heal. My sister, her mouth open in the middle of my brain. Her mouth open in the middle of history.

The house overturned by a cry, the house undone: a nursery rhyme, a photo, a jewelry box. Gold weighs on the back of my mother's neck, chokes her fingers; she dolls herself up, presents herself to the world, piles up her sorrows at the bottom of her drawers alongside the fabrics, the stories, the squares of musk, dried lavender.

We felt the inert guilt of well-off girls. The extent of our madness belongs to those who were not forced to stay in touch with material life, those who had no choice but to keep one foot on the ground. We'd enjoyed the luxury of destroying ourselves with lightning speed, of damaging ourselves to the point of extinction, the luxury of disappointment, waste, and flat generosity, the taste for ransacking and ease. Something exploded in my head. I may well dig myself out of the hole, but I keep one leg dangling in the void.

"A Montrealer, a real little Montrealer," my mother repeats, as if to drive me deeper into the country where she wasn't born.

from which she wasn't borne away

I can't remember the first time I thought of running away from home, but what's always been clear is that my desire wasn't so much for my parents' absence as for the annihilation of their suffocating love that robbed me of myself, the annihilation of this Mediterranean love, this Jewish love, this Sephardic and preventive suffocation laden with a guilt that precedes the massacre and is mixed with the refusal to admit to being Arab, Berber, Moroccans who left Algeria to be on the right side of the decrees, an immense love that threatens to devour me, a love brought to the world like a hand brought to heaven or bread to the mouth, a love of unavowable despair, of accelerated time that swells and cracks at the seams, that solidifies matter and fills the gaps until the dislocation—dislocution—of the belly of the head of the mouth, filling the void stuffing the silence everything force-feeding the belly the head the mouth until it's too much, until the crusts are expelled, the collapse of the heart, the appearance of the black hole, force-feeding in the hope that I'll become a well-integrated, disintegrated little white girl with no accent or any trace of the abandoned continent, a little white girl who'll be seen slipping away toward a dream the name of which we dare not utter, nor suspect of collapsing, not so much out of ignorance as out of a denial necessary for survival, for without this denial all these migrations, all these ambitions, all this work would have been as futile as the little boy's screaming next to his mother and sister, of their two bodies pierced by the same stray bullet, the same French bullet, fired a century ago in the medina of Fez, transmitted to depressed flesh by orphaned bodies, the hole around which my cells were organized in my mother's womb, now a prosthesis holds my heart and lungs which threaten to leak into my intestines, a prosthesis instead of this hole the name of which I deny and which orients my ungrateful escape.

Every place carries the phantom of fantasies disappointed by that place. I wonder if our parents, watching their daughters fall ill, felt that same suffocation faced with the continent's promises. I fail at health, wake up in the sweat of rigged interrogations, electroshocks, cold rooms. This is where I begin, in the mud of dreams, where it screams against the light. I won't heal. I refuse to accept that flaws are only acceptable in view of a potential success story or a memory brought back to the surface. I'm wary of anything that fixes me.

The smart little dog gets beaten and I have to watch. My body is multiplying, and I can no longer distinguish the spectrum from the flesh, the pain from the hologram. I've already been through winters during which I've had to remain silent, like trees whose sap slows down, or certain unicellular algae which, during the cold seasons, retract into a nucleus. I survived like a tardigrade, emptying myself of water and sealing off my cells. I lie down on a warm stone. I wait for my teeth to fall out.

This morning, fires devour the Chouf forests, the woods where I found the timbre of my voice, where I buried my organs. A friend writes to me: *this country is disappearing*. The ravaged earth, I feel it inside me, in my chest and my nerves that crackle down to my legs, down to my powerless hands. I'm not alone in my sorrow. There are many of us, washed by insomnia, developing cancer, reeling from devastation, stammering incantations to try to put things back together. I don't belong anywhere, I'm attached to places that tear me away, that recognize me: the charred cedars of Deir al-Qamar, the black pebbled banks, the red dust of the Ourika. Tough bramble and flat landscapes, where nature gets stripped bare to offer a capacious breath. I inhabit the world's dryness, the anguish of the cracked earth and the thirsts to come.

Migrant dreams come to die inside me. My grandmother calls to warn me: *a curse, a curse, I tell you*. The silences are interwoven, it's impossible to find the thread now, even a trace of the story that brought us here. Names have been erased along with languages and beaches. Ghost languages, ghost beaches, the shores are eroding and I have nothing to say. I embody the failure of the places where I move forward. I speak to the child I won't have. I speak to this child who is me. I am perfectly sedimentary. I never stop giving birth to myself.

It's a story about disappearance. I've only collected a few snippets: as soon as I mention a place, everyone falls silent. I was born of this silence, this hernia of history, a dislocation, the hole between breath and hunger.

I inherit a nostalgia that doesn't belong to me, the nostalgia of an image: a fig tree, a dog at dawn. I try to hold on to bits and pieces, but everything slips out of my hands. I'll end by keeping quiet. I have no story. I've been told nothing, only that there were displacements, escapes, rapes, assassinations, the Crémieux Decree and madness like a crack that was barely visible at first, then widened until it became a chasm, until there was nothing left to break.

There's what's left behind and what catches up to us. It takes perspective to distinguish between them. What seems motionless sometimes approaches very slowly and then, without us realizing, grabs us. It snaps at us like a trap, like a jaw, and we're caught.

I clench my fists, dig my fingernails into my palms, walk through huge, ghostly houses full of cardboard boxes, mirrors, and old candy for grandchildren who will never be born, garages overflowing with useless objects, living rooms with their marble tables and out-of-tune pianos, sumptuous, empty houses on sumptuous, empty streets, where the walls are decorated with photos of suicidal children smiling with their diplomas in hand or standing on a swing, I want to rip open these houses of infinite sadness, make their viscera visible for all to see; I want everyone to bear witness to the reverse side of fantasy and the terrible hollowness that now reigns in these homes, this other cul-de-sac of capitalism and alienation, this clutter which is the opposite of love and abundance, and this debt which is the debt of all the children of immigrants, the obligation to be happy, which is to say, the obligation to be as white as possible.

Perhaps madness can hear the static of everything that runs through our veins. How many more imperceptible vibrations will pass through my temples before a tumor grows in my brain like a galactic center or a peach pit? Data is heating up the ocean floor. Seahorses bathe in our preferences, our shopping carts, our interests, our speculations, our news, our speeches, our credit, our purchases. Zero one one zero zero one one one zero. I'm an algorithm, I'll remain one long after the machine stops working. The grids tell me to find a face. They detect mine and embellish it: my skin becomes paler, my eyelashes grow longer. Further on, suspicious features are identified and arrests multiply. I try a filter with cat ears to fine tune our eugenics. The wind fragments the ice floes and my back is in knots. My madness accuses the world. I'll always have this hole in my head to annihilate the entire universe, to forget, far from gardens, far from love, a sorrow so vast that it becomes the sky itself, the air, the ground. After the rain, after the icemelt, there are still the furrows, the gouged houses vomited into the river, and still we rebuild, because there is no other place than this land of olive trees, bamboo, dung, and plastic, no other water than the one that gorges itself on packaging and piss-soaked rags. A radioactive cloud soars over dunes, mountains, radon mines and Saturday souks, penetrates fruits, clothes, and dawn prayers. On the other side of the desert, women are already birthing jellyfish.

Each fall is a gift that reveals the fragility of structures. That's the eroticism of storms. Last night, I dreamt I was in a movie theater, where they were announcing that a city was burning. I dreamed of an infinite fall that bent the very fabric of time. I dreamed in a language the music of which is still in my marrow.

From the moment the threshold is crossed, from the moment I pass over to the far side of the horizon, I stretch and gravitate irresistibly toward the dark center: I enter a liquid world, an aquatic time, thick as a lava flow.

LETTER

Their love signifies that neither can see the being of the other but only a wound and a need to be ruined. No greater desire exists than a wounded person's need for another wound.

GEORGES BATAILLE, TR. BRUCE BOONE

My pussy wrote a thesis on colonialism

NONAME

I ADDRESS THE MAN and the province and the nation
I address you   you   all of you
    who besiege cities like women
                                        with eyes closed
    leaving a part of you behind

Again and again, I cling to the faces of aging men as if they were an idea of Europe, of integration. It's the same flirtatiousness, the same rot, the same perfume, wrinkles, musk, while the dead-end life and duck lips pronounce the name of some capital. I cling to these disappointing hands, they give me oysters, which I eat and throw up into the restaurant toilet. Someone asks me if I've already killed myself, asks what's wrong. They're all looking for the hole, a loophole to enter, clumsy cock bumps against soft thigh and my body closes up, it starts with the throat, the silent rage, the sewn mouth, love's collapse. I emerge in the bed of a writer who whispers to me, *it's too late you're too old to die young.*

A doctor explains to me that my brain is prone to obsession, that I need to be cautious, careful with exercise, diet, human relationships, it's genetic, he says, it's linked to perfectionism, to millennia-old deficiencies, a starved memory engraved on nerves that buzz on alert. I think of the skeletons of the homosexual couple buried hand in hand centuries ago, then exhumed by archaeologists in a Modena necropolis. I'm thinking of the beavers who go crazy and start destroying everything if they hear a water leak they can't locate. I'm a beaver, I scratch to the bone, the hole is narrow and I dig deep, it's to exhume my skeleton, which holds no one's hand.

You may well say *cattle*, *outsider*, but their eyes are full of an urgency that escapes you. Something that frightens you as it flees. Every disorder is a threat to suffering beings. For a long time, you preferred constellations within reach, a masterable world. You've strangled what resists you, ignored the languages of the places you trample on, whose names you don't pronounce. By denying fascism, by playing on the instinct to flee, you've precipitated your mythologies. It wasn't a struggle, but a return to the land. It wasn't a hatred of the other but a shame of oneself, and there's nothing more dangerous than people who choke down their wounds.

By imitating you, I stifle something that belongs to me. I eat the leftovers, the world marries your ease. You learn slowly, everything accommodates you. When faces, concrete, and homelands come into friction, fanning the flames, you realize what this world is, what it defends, what it reproduces. It's late already, and we're so far from love, so far from avowal.

On the radio, the Prime Minister apologized, he said *yes, it happened,* and there were bursts of applause. You wondered what to do with your guilt, how to admit the wrong, smother the pain, you said *reparations* and waited for someone to comfort you.

You're funded by the arts council and congratulated for asking the question of legacy. You circle your disappearance. You have nothing to declare at the border. You ask for nothing, foreign to your own satiety. You love your province, its soft, monopolizing myth, its museums of sincere poverty. Your inherited arrogance, handed down through centuries of power, exudes the self-evidence of those who give their names to the territories they land in. Clinging to winter like laughter to death, you repeat the myths of the charmers, the fur traders, the water carriers, your little drop of indigenous blood. The same blood that varnishes your antique furniture, where you let me in, saying, *welcome*. I'll question your hospitality, suspect it's transactional. I'll shit on your provinces, your refrains, your cowardice, the little Nazis who warm their hands in the historic church of your capital while you wax on about democracy, minority governments, great culture. I'll shit on your failure, your ambition, your linguistic anxiety, your tests of values and your death-blue eyes. In your geometry, which is the world's very own, my survival is a threat you quickly choke off, like a child's caprice.

In the basement of your house, the basement of history, under the dances, the parties, the shared meals, I played the fuckable fool to excuse my ambition, I learned to get around your clumsiness with secret maneuvers, to shut my mouth before I overflowed. One man tells me to make an effort to be marketable. All the men who have taken advantage of me end up giving me literature classes. I chose this mediocrity. It was a way of going on vacation. It all leaves me with a sharp pain in my pelvis. At night, I take my medication.

I desired you to the point of contempt, cherished your flippancy to the point of eating the moldy compost that enables it. I broke my teeth on the roads that ensured that it was easy for you to go out into the world, to circulate in space, the conditions of a blinding ease, the self-certainty of a proprietor. I'm not playing innocent, I've caused destruction, and the destructions that made me, I went into them willingly. It's not you I blame, it's not me, but all the things that fail through us. You struggle to decipher the exiles that construct me. In the south they murder, and the south keeps rising, soon it will come knocking at our doors. Will you be able to stop yourself from spelling my name then?

I won't talk to you about romance, but about the impulse that propels and shatters us, the gesture by which life, in order to go on, tears away from itself. I talk to you about the rotten smell rising from the flower's sex, the animal frightened by a rustling that's too close, I'm not talking about seduction but voracity—at dawn I bring the damp earth to my mouth, it's a madness as wide and indomitable as the sky, I reorganize my whole life around it, I must remain attentive to the perilous hours. The void around which I compose myself is vitality, it's life itself—it's the birthplace of galaxies. I've embraced the devastation, and laugh in spite of it all.

The separation of bodies is a primary wound, a condition of survival. I come back to you, press my palm against yours, as if to confirm an insurmountable distance. I peel away the layers, reaching the crack that runs through us, the crack that marks the land I leave behind, the lacks from which I learn to love. We are lives borrowed from the torrents that overflow us, and if I approach you, it's to replay this separation that is the proof of all life. I'm looking for the sacred moment when a creature rips the membrane that protected it from the world, when the cells tear away from each other. Even if it means becoming your autoimmune disease, your symbiotic parasite:

a tailor-made ravaging, even more dangerous than a foreign body. I've reached my monstrosity. I no longer expect you to recognize me.

HERE I AM,
A DULL TRANSPLANT

. . . if a sea cucumber is starving, instead of rolling over
it just eats itself, gradually becoming smaller and smaller

JUSTINE E. HAUSHEER

I don't have anything to nourish me: I eat myself

CLARICE LISPECTOR, TR. JOHNNY LORENZ

I SWALLOW THE KEYS to my underground doors
I arrive at the word

I want to ditch enthusiasm to undress
my body is always late
to mourning I look at myself I take a photo of myself
I erase everything I tell myself it can't be erased
there must be a dimension of faces lost
under the smooth image you control yourself I always want
something of what disgusts me my blood overflows
I know how to claim a place
but if I escape it's in order to spill out

I doubt the stories   the madness of centuries
ossifies on the back of my neck
demands to know   what crime we are
made of   to be so afraid   of what questions us
                                                            of what constitutes us

here I am, a dull transplant in your country
in the regret of a river and the cult of that regret
    in contempt for defeats and ambitions   a papier-mâché
capital   where laws are cemented
                                        where cobblestones choke fear
where my friend's mosque bleeds   without commemoration

facing the window I spread my legs   bodies cross the border repressed bodies torn away   from each other locked up in cold rooms   I shiver on the other side of the wall   your tongue climbs my breasts   I can't carry our dead on my back   when it's not thirst it's an electric fence   a blank bullet   salt water that scratches the skin   those bodies leave nothing behind   once they're fished out, they get buried under stones   no number on the headstone   spirits turn the army denies   their existence   the families   comrades stand and wait   frozen in time   in air contaminated   by the military gazes that separate   erase   dry up bodies and days at the thoracic root

my palms sweat pressed against the brick
the officer's hands touch me   his colleague repeats
are you sure   you were born   here?
          next to me my one-night-stand   a white British guy
without a visa   smiles wryly   they won't ask him a thing
the agent continues   rifling through my fear
feels it   revels in it
                                        I tell him it's not mine
it was palmed off on me   this fear
I inherited it like my memory, like all desire
the agent continues   pats the length of my body
finds nothing in my pockets   only the salt
                                                            of a crossed sea

assimilation: a need for love: an imperative to erase: it's the price to pay: I cut out my tongue to cross this threshold: one always pays for what the other flees: masters are just another kind of sorrow: to subjugate: to smooth out in order to exist: good intentions erase history: protocols are established: administrative sadness: it's the order of things: what swallows us: all bodies mixed together

they tell me to clear my mind but it's
    the emptiness that clears me out
they tell me that admitting is enough to find resolution
    I no longer dare believe
in gestures   naming things   saving face
    the whole city washes its hands   a hundred times a day

we shared the war
    maybe the deepest of ties
a reciprocal excavation
perhaps war is an intimacy that hesitates
    perhaps bodies never know each other as well
as when they're at war

each lost love shapes my body like a land of exile
                I sculpt myself in the negative space of your word
I ask for the privilege of adopting the trees' rhythm
        may the bombarded faces forgive me
colors hallucinate me   I try so hard not to look for you in
the streets that know nothing about me
I'm no longer able to cry   I eat   I try to mimic the
gestures   of the living   I know nothing of love
    I listen to what sings at the site of the cut

pink algae grows on snow
at the tops of mountains   they survive delicate melts
    tuck in mummified children   instead of writing you
a love letter   I travel through scarred places
            where trees watch over the smothered earth
    my hatreds bind me
        I'm unable to write tenderness
I know that all faces are beautiful when one lingers on them
no   I won't speak to you of   sweetness
    so it can remain secret
                                    so it can survive
if I show it   if I name it I risk   its destruction
I have inherited
the fear   of those whose place is fragile
this sheltering silence   is a last resort

the boat approaches   splits the surface   of the lake grinds
the reflected landscape   the man smiles
and asks   if he can help us
he wants to clarify the situation   make sure we're
in the right place   his gaze slides over our skin
I say I'm home   that my family lives here
he looks at us again   *ah right, your family*   *who's your family*
    asks me to spell my name   puts me back   apologizes
if you'd been strangers   *I'd have asked you to leave*

once you've crossed the threshold become a
    housekeeper   nanny   handywoman
live in their eyes   learn their houses   knowing
you'll never be like them   at home   in cabs
overqualified immigrant doctors   architects
know the city better than I do
        teach me to breathe in blind spots

I've withdrawn from the world I live in a cave
I am an orifice
the rain makes the garden tremble I am waiting to become
a plant a mineral
can you molt from another body another voice
molt from a glance
can you eat the molting of your sadness
touch the heart the mystical vibration
before paying the bills burning the letters washing the dishes

there's no folklore to take refuge in
too many displaced bodies
I soon realized we'd have to live like this
from one election to the next
in flaccid hopes shrugging our shoulders
watching documentaries
bearing witness to the yawning century
pressing on our hearts
turning the page
showing our credentials letting ourselves feel moved
by a season by a speech
raising awareness about plastic
congratulating diversity committees
special clauses
that rename what doesn't change
swallowing history swallowing vomiting
decolonial
vomiting every last drop
one vertebra at a time
returning to the protozoan liquid state
living like this
letting go without blaming the world for the love
we never received
that we could never give ourselves

I will not fill the gap

only the gap imitates nothing

ZHOR

Our fate is decided among words without weight or color, gestures that no memory, no clay, no reflection can capture. With us, outside of us. I listened; one can always listen. The other world is us, too, always us.

MOHAMMED DIB

But there was that hunger; it followed me.

RENEE GLADMAN

THE MOURNING WOMEN WAIL in the street, I avoid looking out the window, I cover the mirrors to slow my decomposition. It's a fragile day; a gust of wind would be enough to dismember me. In the room that serves as my bedroom, a man died of AIDS, surrounded by his friends. His bed was in the same place as mine, its head against the brick wall, its foot toward the door. *He was an eccentric*, says my neighbor from the balcony next door, *a flamboyant fag, a crazy architect, he often brought lovers home, he threw big parties*. Then she leans toward me, with that way people have of leaning toward you when they're about to say something horrible: *He got sick, but he asked for it*. According to her, he's the one who hid an electric watch in the wall. But I've been here so long that I don't hear the plaster ringing anymore, only the neighbors knocking above, below, next door, so my walls still shake, and I guess sadness works a bit like that, after a while you don't hear it anymore, the alarm becomes like the air, like the sky, until someone hits a surface and you emerge for a moment from this dazzling madness, get out of the house to extract yourself before plunging back in, get out, quickly, while it's still possible and even if the alarm remains lodged in your skull, get out and walk the same streets, changing trajectories, walking the alarm like a dead dog at the end of its leash and letting your house collapse behind you.

I searched, I forgot what I'd lost, even the hollow left behind by that loss had lost its contours, I no longer recognized anything, not even a shape that might have been able to fill it, soon it became impossible to know if I was looking for love, a glove, a cat, a tongue, a child, the more I searched, the more I forgot, my steps sunk me into oblivion and oblivion into this loss, and I wondered if it was even mine, if I hadn't been infected by an endemic, ancestral loss.

I'd already grown old by the time I walked through the city, I could see it in the faces of the strangers smoking on the sidewalk, in how they let me pass—normally the jostling multiplies to such an extent that I end up believing I'm invisible. I moved forward, distraught, into this aging, until I wondered if we weren't already dead, because in the streets there was no trace of our existence, only the terrible hope of finding you where we'd said goodbye, finding you like a grave or a river, finding you again, even if it meant becoming one of those animals that keep returning to the same place to lay eggs, to drink, to die.

In cafés, buses, and departure halls, fascism takes hold with a red hat on its head. We look away out of politeness. Cordially, that's how it manages to sit down, to take a seat. I wear myself out, trying to keep my eyes open; I drain out my blood, my thoughts, my very fatigue.

My mother's body unravels the moment I detach myself from the continent. The ligaments that served as her net have given way, her bladder lowers into her vagina. One by one, she gives birth to her organs. We don't fail from the same place. Our bodies disassemble to go back in time. The hole is an organ, and the organ creates the function. I have a prosthesis under my heart, like a dam retaining the sea.

I fall asleep on the plane, dreaming of swans and burning cathedrals. A lost language soothes me, cradles my throat. It's the language of tenderness and secrets, plots, whispered conversations, the kind we prefer to keep hidden from children. I fly over the drowned, the ships spotted and then left behind by the *Guardia Civil*, I show my passport, and a woman gets shot in the head after being turned away by a state officer.

Childhood cracks me apart. I said I came from nowhere, that I had no country, no town, only a charred forest, only dunes, rocks and tide. I keep quiet, too many things in my mouth, fingers, accents, geographies. I cling to the trace of loss. It's a period of mourning without an object, a transmitted silence that contracts like a heart or a disease. There will be no trial. I will escape into a language without finding refuge there.

Cement has filled the mouths, coated the mountains. In a village of blackbirds and red earth, a woman learns to count her children's ages. The grey cat gave birth in the garden, after which she was not seen again for weeks. When she returned, she had no litter; the janitor says she must have eaten her young. Madness is hidden away here, but it catches up with us. An itinerant woman hobbles in place, rocking asymmetrically, as if sinking into invisible mud. She clutches a torn plastic bag with one hand, covers one ear with the other, her mouth distorted by voices no one else can hear. Careful, my father tells me, or you'll end up in Berrechid, where they send the lunatics before forgetting all about them. My father's stiff shoulders gut me. I'd like to caress the dark circles under his eyes, pour over his body the warm sand of the country he left behind. My father is shrinking, soon I'll be carrying him on my forearms, cradling him, laying him down in a citrus garden. In the meantime, I eat the crumbs of his memory, of his country. I keep the name Berrechid in my mouth, tracing it with my lips and tongue, making it my silent litany.

I look the same in every town, the knotted muscles of my face losing the habit of speaking the language, some of which I have to unearth in the sleeping parts of my mouth. Crossing the douar, I recognize writing: the caves, the nights of warming bodies, the iron scent of childbirth, the numbers counted out in the other's tongue. It is here that I learn not to lower my gaze.

I dream that my grandfather, a Frenchman who married an Algerian woman, is a collaborator. He says: "If you can sell the name, you sell the name." I ask him about it, and he tells me that she was the love of his life. That she died of AIDS, after a contaminated transfusion in a Paris hospital. Guibert said that to have AIDS is to experience the nudity of one's own blood. French blood undressed this woman from the inside. In her letters, she wrote: *I've come for treatment, but please don't say anything to the girl*, words traced with a fountain pen in perfect calligraphy, drawn up in blotting paper where the ink stains spread like a tumor in the skull or tar on the sea. My grandmother's emaciated body, rubbed with argan oil and covered with rose petals, shrinks, recedes, becomes the silence in my father's mouth.

The wadi is filled with the icy waters of the Atlas Mountains. The melting ice uncovers the bodies of explorers and drowns those of peasant families. A man digs in the earth and tells me: *I'm going to find the whale underneath.*

Many women leave the area with their lives on their backs, to make the crossing, to be neither here nor there, to sink with their names hanging from their necks, to go down into the waters or under the earth of Oujda's forests. Some say *irregular entries*, others that bodies *disappear* at the border, others that they *fly away* or get destroyed *without name or face*, a few frantic hands lift the stones in search of a trace. As for me, I do nothing, I move into death as into fresh water, I think of the strength of everything that has been taken away and I get high as much to celebrate as to exact my revenge.

They thought they could run away from their history, and they were right, but now I'm stuck with the void instead of history, I keep telling myself that it doesn't matter, that we have to kill the very idea of origin, that it's impossible to go back to the source of things, unless we go all the way back to a pre-species, before humans differentiated themselves from jellyfish and dragonflies.

My landscape is a hostile place, ravaged by craters, the imprints left by vanished love and imposed love, the gorged mouth, the grasp disguised as a gift, the residual guilt of a body breaking off. I've rediscovered my arch in limestone places. I tear myself away, stick to the rocks, become stone, sap, sky.

Ancient songs, shock waves pass through me, translating the hole just beneath my heart, ready to swallow it. The excavation of deep music returns me to my anonymity. I am matter, its dissolution, its overflow. Like all love, I'm born of a first spasm, a pulsing between excess and lack.

In the earliest myths, jealous gods gave birth through their mouths. They vomit birth. Devouring in reverse. I climb the mountainside. I burn my shoes to enter a forest we might believe, mistakenly, we belong to. The forest won't forgive us. The cedars protect me, their wounded trunks strengthened by dull length. Hungry animals cry out in the mist. I hear my heart beating underground. I find my hands in the ruins. It is here that I give birth to myself.

I peel clementines on the café table and eat them, crying. A sticky mixture of pulp and saliva runs down my chin. Bulls in the streets, the houses barred. Peels and tears pile up on the table, dogs strain to disentangle themselves from seaweed and a drone ejaculates thirty feet up.

I drag my tears to Delphi, where I leave the window open, cry again with the swallows circling in the room, cry as I run my fingers over the engraved marble, cry in the grotto of the oracles, then on the boat that takes me to the island.

I pull mucus out of the inside of my throat, like spit too thick to tear, too massive to swallow, and as I spit my nerves detach, my esophagus, my stomach, my intestines, all the inside comes out, caught in the same gelatinous membrane. My mouth is a vagina, I vomit myself up, the placenta stuffs me, suffocates me, I grab it and try to pull it out with the urgency of asphyxia, blinded by the pain where I sink as if into a frozen lake.

Nausea pulls me out of my nightmares. After hours spent sweating acid, vomiting air, and shitting bile, I look at the map and spot the little niche in Achilles Bay, convinced that's where I must go to abort my mother. On the phone, underneath the tenderness of her voice, there's hope shot like a cannonball, as if you could protect your child from the world, as if you could erase history, its filth, its cowardice, by crossing the Atlantic to settle in the heart of winter, national holidays, and backstage wars.

The bay is a deserted, filthy port, littered with garbage, reeking of piss. Not even a garbage dump. A few seabirds flit about on the surface, between plastic bags and bits of Styrofoam. It was in these waters that Thetis, after throwing her other children into the fire, soaked her son Achilles, pulling him under by the ankle. I love this story, because it shows that the grip is what determines fragility. We suffer where we've been held, loved, squeezed. It's where we die, too, when the tide goes out and the world cuts through us. The hole exists because it was once something other than a hole.

What we bear witness to weighs on us. It's not a weight we can measure; we can't measure all experience. What I've seen accumulates in the depths of my body, the strata pile up, interlock, sediment, my bones are engraved with lies. I repeat that there is no origin, to convince myself: a gesticulation in an indeterminate plasma. I repeat: I give birth to myself. I repeat it in order to exist, to dissolve in a different way.

Voices pass through me the moment the star's heart collapses. The sky is beautiful above the corpses, I turn off the music to listen. Children play like birds in the dust. They will be the drowned in the great droughts. A woman sings:

When the horizon rises like a tide of fire, will you forgive me?

When a number has replaced your face, when your cry turns to coral, will you forgive me?

Do you know that you can die from a lack of narration?

I met a woman who repeated her name, twisting it until her hands bled. I knew a woman who put plane leaves on the eyes of the dead. I'm going to tell you about the most beautiful moment of my life. It was the summer of the crisis, of families shot at the Hungarian borders and the unfathomable grief that propelled me into someone else's childhood, in the red mountains from which we could see the sea and its engulfed suns. For weeks I spoke to no one. Months spent forgetting the sound of my own voice. Then came autumn, then winter, birds intoxicated by figs, grenades ripped open at the foot of trees, abandoned tanks and ferocious downpours on the tin. I walked alone, for a long time, on the mountain. I listened to the cedars. One day I noticed a blue tarp on the opposite hill. Broken bottles, a dying fire. And a man. He jumped when he saw me. He was afraid of me, I of him. He must have thought I was going to report him: the town was trying to flush out the refugees, accusing them of burglary. I was afraid he'd cross over, that he'd come at me, that he'd rape me. We looked at each other like deer. Then he raised his hands and I raised mine. We backed away, very slowly, in opposite directions, until we disappeared from each other's sight.

THE UNINHABITABLE ORIFICE

THERE'S A MOUTH at the center of the earth
words foods languages enter and exit the mouth
winds animals trees enter and exit the earth enter and exit the mouth
the mouth dissolves the body   it's the primary orifice
the uninhabitable orifice
the border-hole history's sex
its final point that approaches to engulf
sink to the core   return to water
return to the void
my body orbits the void
history revolves around the void
I open   my mouth
I vomit the egg intact   I vomit eyes planets
women's riddled bodies
the tumors riddling women's bodies
I'm going to enter the stage take off all the layers reach the center the mouth which is the sex of the world the shore which precedes and waits for me
I open my mouth
in the beginning a woman vomits   in the beginning a vagina dilates with the throat and pupil the earth cracks it's an overdose it's the creation of the world it's a cry that surpasses itself it's the secret that saves us it's the silence of

mothers who squeeze daughters between their thighs it's meat
ripped off the bone the dazzled spasm it's not said it's the
nothing I say   I say nothing
that's what I touch
I possess my disappearance
I apologize to the forest
summons the unheard-of   Oran Oka   Hô Chi Minh City
Kahnawà:ke   Deir al-Qamar
Algiers Annam protectorates
tongues torn out   ghost tongues still swarming
I melt into the walls I'm on the side of extinction
it's a contraction it's the birth of the world torn
from the world
a deformed gesture the tracing of a drowning
I mourn the earth
I see my mother fade, grow old, shine
in inconsolable grief
the scratchings-out are landscapes
I cradle the void   worlds are engendered in my muddy blood
the star collapses, sinking at its center
water finds its way under stone memories
hunger mutates from body to body
flesh rolls begets
pierces devours   an ancestral appetite
the core pulsates inside a dead bird
the stray bullet shimmers under the heart
lodged in interrupted   breaths transmitted falls
the space of one last resistance
and what's left of love will crawl into the clay
to return to the sea

Acknowledgments

The author and translator would like to thank the Nightboat team—Lindsey Boldt, Emily Bark Brown, Morgan Levine, Stephen Motika, Dante Silva, and, especially, their editor Lina Bergamini—for their efforts in making this book a reality.

About Nightboat Books

Nightboat Books, a nonprofit organization, seeks to develop audiences for writers whose work resists convention and transcends boundaries. We publish books rich with poignancy, intelligence, and risk. Please visit nightboat.org to learn about our titles and how you can support our future publications.

The following individuals have supported the publication of this book. We thank them for their generosity and commitment to the mission of Nightboat Books:

Kazim Ali, Anonymous (3), Ava Aviva Avnisan, Jean C. Ballantyne, Rumeli Banik, Will Blythe, Rob Byrnes, V. Shannon Clyne, Theodore Cornwell, Gisela Gamper, Photios Giovanis, Amanda Greenberger, David Groff, Jonathan Groff, Daniel Handler, Sarah Heller, Karen Holtzman, Parag Rajendra Khandhar, Katy Lederer, Shari Leinwand, Daniel Levine, Elizabeth Madans, Ricardo Maldonado, Pooja Mehta, Ethan Mitchell, Caren Motika, Elizabeth Motika, Asker Saeed, The Leslie Scalapino - O Books Fund, Amy Scholder, Eric Suchyta, Benjamin Taylor, Mohan Trivedi, Divya Victor, Jerrie Whitfield & Richard Motika, Clay Williams

This book is made possible, in part, by grants from the New York City Department of Cultural Affairs in partnership with the City Council and the New York State Council on the Arts Literature Program.